P9-CDL-739

Seasons of the Bear

A Yosemite Story

Ginger Wadsworth

ILLUSTRATED BY Daniel San Souci

YOSEMITE CONSERVANCY
Yosemite National Park

In memory of Robert San Souci, who loved Yosemite National Park

YOSEMITE CONSERVANCY®

yosemiteconservancy.org

Yosemite Conservancy's Mission
Providing for Yosemite's future is our passion. We inspire people to support projects and programs that preserve and protect Yosemite National Park's resources and enrich the visitor experience.

Library of Congress Control Number: 2015957027

Cover art by Daniel San Souci
Book design by Nancy Austin

ISBN 978-1-930238-66-4
Printed in China by Toppan Leefung, April 2016

1 2 3 4 5 6 – 20 19 18 17 16

FSC
www.fsc.org

MIX
Paper from
responsible sources
FSC® C104723

YOSEMITE NATIONAL PARK wears winter white.
A hawk searches the high country for food
while Bear stirs below in her cozy den.

Waaah! Waaah! WAAAH!
Bear's newborn cubs yowl.
After Bear licks her babies clean,
she gently hugs them.
Ooh-Ooh-Coo! Ooh-Ooh-Coo!
The twins nurse on milk thicker than cream,
their little motors thrumming until they sleep.

Bear dozes, too.

Bear's babies are growing fast!
One cub jabs the other with his toes.
His brother punches him in the nose.
Wham! Whack!
They pounce on each other
and roll on the ground.
They try to jump on Bear.
She grumbles gently.
Grrrrr.

Bear pokes her nose outside.

Bear slips into the welcoming sun.
She strolls past patches of snow,
leaving paw prints in the damp earth.
Bear sniffs the air.
After months of feeding her babies
but not herself,
Bear is hungry . . . very hungry!
The smell of spring grass tempts her.

But first,
Bear rakes up last year's leaves and pine needles
to build a soft bed.

She hauls one baby outside, then the other, and
    they tumble on the leafy mattress.

Bear wastes no time!
She bites off tender blades of grass.
A curious cub wanders over.
He nibbles some grass.
He chews.
He eats more!
His brother joins the meal.
BURP!
Two copycat cubs are now salad eaters like
    their mother.

Soon Bear knows it is time to move.
She hides her sleepy cubs under a jumble of logs and
    sets off in search of more food.
A creek's water music lulls her babies to sleep.

After their nap,
the twins sneak out to explore.
Melting snow and chunks of ice overflow
    the creek's banks.
Crack! Snap! Whoosh! Roar!
The slushy creek spreads onto the land.
As the icy flow picks up speed,
it washes the cubs away.
They bang into trees,
spin around boulders,
and bump into each other.

They cry *Eeh! Eeh! Eeh!*
Bear splashes through the slush,
clacking her teeth in distress.

Bear yanks each cub onto dry land.
Whap! Whap! Whap!
She swats them for wandering away.

Bear licks the ice off their fur.

IN TUOLUMNE MEADOWS'S wide-open spaces,
Bear and her family munch grass.
Buses and cars pause at the edge of the road
so summer visitors with long lenses can snap
     pictures.
"Ooh, I see a bear," someone shrieks.
"It's two bears!"
"No! Three!" a girl tells her dad.

Three bears vanish into the tall grass
and amble into the shady forest.
"Where did they go?" wonders the girl.
Doors slam.
Motors start up.

It's nearly dark as the bears start to cross a road.
Headlights suddenly brighten the blacktop.
Scree-ee-ee-ee-ch!

Bear's family dashes to the far side of the pavement
just as the speeding car swerves around them.

In the cool of the morning,
Bear nips at two tiny tails
to hurry her cubs up a tree-shaded trail to
    Dog Lake.

Bear's needle-sharp claws splinter a rotting log.
Creamy white grubs squirm.
Long, sticky tongues roll out to gobble up the grubs.

One morning, a large male bear unexpectedly
     appears.
Bear's cubs ladder up a tree,
branch by branch.

Bear faces the newcomer.
A woof rumbles from deep within her throat.
She blows *Ohff! Ohff!*
Bear lowers her head.
She flattens her ears.
The big bear skedaddles,
crashing through the forest like a runaway truck.

Bear calls all clear
Uh! Uh!
until her cubs scramble down.

AUTUMN LEAVES turn orange and gold.
Lightning flashes over the mountaintops.
Thunder claps and rumbles.
Dry grasses rustle.
As always,
Bear is hungry . . . very hungry.
She stands and sniffs for her next meal.

Instead,
Bear smells danger.
Dove-gray smoke billows nearby.
Whoosh!
One tree explodes in flames, then another.
A line of fire dances in the wind.
Crackle! Pop! Sizzle!

Bear turns and barrels through the tall grass,
her cubs hurtling close behind.

A terrified squirrel barks *chick-a-ree-ree*
and scampers up and down a tree.
Deer zigzag through a cloud of smoke.
Red-hot embers twirl in the air.
One stings Bear's nose.
She squeals and hurries on.
Her twins sprint to keep up.

At last, a steady rain slows the wildfire.
Bear prods her cubs into the night.

The cubs start to lag behind.
One nearly tumbles off the trail.
Little legs wobble, and both cubs wail.
Everyone is worn out.

Finally, all three climb up a tree
and dangle their legs over sturdy branches.
They nap.

The smell of smoke lingers,
but Bear smells something new.
Her eyes open.

Bear shimmies down the trunk.
The cubs scurry down, too.
Three bears stand still.
Sniff! Snort! Sniff! Snort!

Then they break into a trot.

A few miles away,
they reach an oak grove.
The cubs scuttle up the biggest tree,
and acorns shake free.
Bear stuffs her mouth.
Her forty-two teeth grind the nuts into gritty mush.
The brothers slide down to join her.
It's time to fatten up!

Dark, wintry clouds drift in.
Snowflakes flutter down,
sticking to Bear and her cubs.
The snow falls faster and swirls every which way.
Soon it's hard to see.

Bear and her cubs waddle into the storm.

She leads them on a well-worn route
used by bears for thousands of years.
The cubs shuffle behind her.
At the entrance to Bear's den,
her twins rush in first.

Bear's head and shoulders squeeze in.
Oomph!
Front claws scrabble on the rocky floor.
Her behind and tail wiggle, then disappear,
followed by her back paws.

Tucked in together in Yosemite National Park,
Bear and her cubs soon fall asleep.
Three heartbeats slow.
Thump! Thuummp! Thuuuuummmp!
A new season begins.

AUTHOR'S NOTE

A question that visitors to Yosemite National Park often ask is, "Do you think I'll see a bear?"

American black bears (*Ursus americanus*) live in many of the forested areas of North America. Some are black, but in Yosemite most are actually brown, blond, or even reddish brown. Males can reach 350 pounds; females are much smaller.

Yosemite's bears are typically born between January and March. At birth, they are blind, nearly hairless, and weigh less than a pound. They rely solely on their mother's rich milk for nourishment until spring, when the family emerges from its den to search for food. Cubs will stay with their mother for about a year and a half, after which they will set out on their own to live a solitary life.

Day and night, older cubs and grown bears dine on grasses, berries, roots, acorns, and soft, white grubs, the protein-rich larvae of beetles. Most of the year, they eat about five thousand calories a day, which would be like a human eating fifteen peanut butter and jelly sandwiches. Large males need more calories than females and young bears.

Bears generally lose weight in the winter when edible plants are hidden under a blanket of snow or are not producing berries or nuts. In the fall, they stuff themselves with as much food as they can find, often eating up to twenty thousand calories a day (up to sixty peanut butter and jelly sandwiches!), to be ready for the lean times ahead.

Bears can run fast, climb trees, and hear extremely well. But smell is a bear's most important sense. Bears will wander, run, slide, and even swim to reach food they smell several miles away. They are incredibly curious and very smart, too. They also have excellent eyesight and see colors, so they have learned to recognize and rip open ice chests, backpacks, and grocery bags in their search for something to eat. This has drawn bears closer to people, where they can easily become too comfortable in the park's campgrounds and picnic areas, as they rummage for food. This can put bears at risk.

To keep bears healthy and safe, Yosemite National Park has a human-bear management program. Signs are placed along roads to remind drivers to slow down and watch for bears. Some bears have been outfitted with GPS collars so the National Park Service can track their daily movements.

No one wants a bear to eat a banana, a tuna sandwich, or a hunk of cheese. That's for humans! Visitors must store their drinks, food, scented items, and even ice chests in the bear-proof containers placed throughout the park. Backpackers use smaller, portable canisters. All trash must go into sealed garbage cans. Rangers patrol campgrounds and trails year-round to remind everyone of these important rules. Yosemite Conservancy supports the program by paying for bear-proof storage, providing bear-tracking tools, and by educating visitors about the importance of this effort.

After many years, the program is working! With less available human food, bears are foraging more naturally and staying farther away from developed areas and campsites. It's a win-win situation for them and for the visitors who want to observe *wild, healthy* bears in Yosemite National Park. Only three hundred to five hundred black bears live in Yosemite's 750,000 acres. Consider yourself lucky if you do indeed spot one.

ACKNOWLEDGMENTS

Caitlin Lee-Roney, wildlife biologist, Resources Management and Science Division, National Park Service in Yosemite National Park

Kate McCurdy, manager of Sedgwick Reserve, Santa Barbara, California

Jeffrey Trust, park ranger, Division of Interpretation and Education, National Park Service in Yosemite National Park